bindi
Wildlife Adventures

BOOK
5

A WHALE
OF A TIME

bindi
Wildlife Adventures

A WHALE
OF A TIME

Bindi Irwin

with Chris Kunz

sourcebooks
jabberwocky

Copyright © Australia Zoo 2010
Cover photograph © Getty Images
Cover and internal design by Christabella Designs
Cover and internal design © 2011 Sourcebooks, Inc.

Published by Sourcebooks Jabberwocky, an imprint of Sourcebooks, Inc.
P.O. Box 4410, Naperville, Illinois 60567-4410
(630) 961-3900
Fax: (630) 961-2168
www.jabberwockykids.com

First published by Random House Australia in 2010.

Library of Congress Cataloging-in-Publication data is on file with the publisher.

Source of Production: Versa Press, East Peoria, Illinois, USA
Date of Production: July 2011
Run Number: 15440

Printed and bound in the United States of America.
VP 10 9 8 7 6 5 4 3 2 1

Dear Diary,

I am so lucky to live in a part of the world where all you have to do to see the most amazing humpback whales is jump in a boat. When my English friends came to visit, I took them out for a once in a lifetime whale-watching experience. But the day didn't turn out quite as planned. Although we saw some beautiful whales, Andy got really seasick. And things became a lot more complicated and awful when we discovered an oil spill...

Bindi

CHAPTER ONE

Caitlin and Andy Blake, twelve-year-old twins, were blindfolded in the backseat of the car. It was a winter's day in Queensland, but because it was Queensland, the sun was still shining and the weather was (balmy). The car was traveling along a single lane highway, passing through beautiful Australian bushland. It was really very picturesque but, sadly, not if you were wearing a blindfold.

"How much longer now, Bindi?" asked Andy, who was trying to sneak a peek from the bottom of his blindfold. He was a gangly, dark-haired boy, whose legs and arms sprawled in every direction. His twin sister seemed much more contained. She was shorter, with blond hair and a natural confidence. They were like night and day.

Bindi was sitting in the front passenger's seat. She glanced over at her mum, Terri, who was driving.

Terri raised two of her fingers to indicate they were about two minutes away.

"Not long, Andy. Hey, and no peeking!"

Caitlin was outraged. "What? Can he see where we're going? That's not fair!" She whacked her brother on the arm.

"Owww, I can*not*. Keep your hair on!" Andy hit his sister back.

Terri glanced in the rearview mirror. "You two, be nice to each other. We're almost there."

A few moments later the car pulled into the parking lot at Mooloolaba Wharf.

Bindi consulted her watch. "Right on time, Mum. Nice work. Okay, you two, time to take off the blindfolds."

Caitlin and Andy pulled off the blindfolds and paused for a few seconds to adjust to the light. The twins lived in England but were visiting Australia with their parents, who were speaking at an environmental conference in Brisbane today. They were old family friends of the Irwins, and this was the first time the twins had been to Australia. Bindi had enthusiastically offered to spend the day showing the twins around.

Terri grinned as the kids piled out of the car. "Well, I have to get back to the zoo, so have a terrific time today, kids," she said from the driver's seat. "Bindi, remember that Derek will drop you back off at the zoo after—"

"Mum!" Bindi interrupted. "Don't spoil the surprise!"

"I was going to say after*ward*," replied Terri. She waved good-bye and drove off.

"So where are we exactly?" Caitlin asked, looking around and noticing that they were near the water's edge.

"At Mooloolaba Wharf," answered Bindi. "Just in time to jump aboard a boat to go—"

"Whale watching?" Andy finished her sentence, sounding concerned.

He was looking at an impressive catamaran moored at the wharf with the name *Steve's Whale One* emblazoned on the side.

"Good guess, Andy!" answered Bindi, not noticing his frown. "This is the time of year when humpback whales travel up the east coast to warmer waters where they can reproduce, and that catamaran over there is going to take us on a fantastic cruise—"

Again, Andy interrupted. "On the water?"

Caitlin giggled and gave him a sympathetic smile. "You better tell her, Andy."

Bindi looked confused. "Tell me what?"

Andy gave his twin a pointed look. "There's nothing to tell, Bindi."

Caitlin didn't agree. "Well, Andy isn't what you call 'robust' when he gets anywhere near a boat..."

Bindi didn't understand.

Caitlin was enjoying herself. "He's more bookish. You know, very good at languages, not so good with travel sickness."

Bindi felt terrible. "Oh, Andy, do you get seasick? I'm so sorry. I didn't realize. I thought a day out on the water—"

"Look, it's fine. I haven't been on

a boat for years. I've probably grown out of getting seasick anyway," suggested Andy optimistically.

"Are you sure?" Bindi asked. "We can do something else. Maybe go for a bushwalk instead?"

Andy glanced at his sister, who was trying to hide her smile, and replied firmly, "Bindi, I would love to go whale watching. We'll have a wonderful time, as long as the weather doesn't become...really stormy. Like a cyclone, for instance," he finished, looking smug.

Caitlin's eyes widened. "The weather forecast is fine for today, isn't it, Bindi? On the news back home we've heard about some of the"—she gulped—"cyclones that have pounded the Australian coastline."

"Not to mention the shark attacks, all the poisonous spiders and snakes…" added Andy.

"And the British tourists that g-get lost in the outback," finished Caitlin, now looking totally spooked.

Bindi glanced from one twin to the other. At first she thought they were joking—but both of them looked genuinely frightened! "Come on, you two, Australia's the best country in the world. It's not scary at all! Follow me." She headed off in the direction of the wharf.

The twins looked at each other a little nervously.

Andy said, "Remember, Bindi feeds crocodiles and cuddles up to pythons in her spare time. She has a completely different idea of 'scary' to us."

"Thanks, Andy. That makes me feel a whole lot better!" Caitlin grimaced as she hurried to catch up to their fearless Australian friend.

CHAPTER TWO

The three kids were super lucky. Today they had *Steve's Whale One*, Australia Zoo's specially designed whale-watching catamaran, all to themselves. As they scrambled up the gangplank, Captain Derek Washington was waiting to greet them.

"G'day, Bindi," said Captain Washington. "These two must be your British mates?" He gave them both a vigorous handshake. A big burly man with ruddy cheeks, he looked like the perfect seaman, right down to his starched white uniform and cap. "Welcome aboard. We're due to leave in five minutes, so I need to do the safety checks."

Andy looked concerned. "Yes, good idea. Don't let us keep you from checking that the boat is safe. I guess you'd be checking that there are enough life jackets on board and life preservers in case anyone falls in, and that there are definitely no leaks anywhere?"

14

Captain Washington cast a quick sideways glance at Bindi, who grinned at him. "Yes, boyo, that's exactly the type of safety check I'll be doing," he said, patting him on the shoulder. "Now, why don't the three of you get yourself a nice drink and then come up to the bridge. That's where I'll be steering from, and you'll get the best views from there as we motor out through the heads."

Caitlin was thrilled. Her earlier nervousness had now disappeared. "Su-*perb*."

Sadly, the same could not be said for Andy, who already seemed a little green around the gills.

"Once we start moving, there will be less rocking, Andy. I promise. In the meantime, let's get you a juice," Bindi said, taking Andy's arm and leading her guests into the main cabin.

Ten minutes later, the catamaran was cruising through the canals of Mooloolaba, on its way out to the open ocean. The three kids had pride of place on the bridge, with Captain Washington at the helm. He radioed through to the coastguard. "Coastguard Mooloolaba, we'll be whale watching 15 nautical miles radius east of Port Cartwright. Our ETA is 1430 hours."

The radio crackled its response. "Roger that, *Whale One*, enjoy your cruise. Over."

Caitlin could not be more excited. "Thanks so, so much for this amazing opportunity, Bindi. I've always, *always* wanted to go whale watching." The water was crystal clear, and the sky was blue. She could already see schools of fish under the water as the boat sped on. It was the perfect day to be on the ocean!

"You'll love it," enthused Bindi. "I've gone out heaps of times but every time I get the same thrill when I see those majestic creatures." She turned to the captain. "Captain Washington, have you seen Ash the humpback lately?"

"She's still cruising around the area," replied the captain. "After their young are born," he explained to the twins, "the whales stay in the warmer waters and nurse their young. They don't return to the Antarctic until the calf has developed enough blubber to keep it alive in the icy climate. And Ash, in particular, seems to have a soft spot for

18

Bindi. She's always eager to come over with her calf and say g'day if she sees Bindi on board." He turned to look over at Andy, who was staring down into his lap, muttering quietly to himself. "How're you going there, mate?"

"Yeah, fine, fine," said Andy, although it was clear he was not feeling fine at all.

"Hey, Andy, focus on a point far on the horizon, and it might stop you from feeling sick," Bindi suggested, trying to be helpful.

Andy looked far from convinced but didn't want to cause a fuss. He reluctantly lifted his head and

looked out toward the horizon...
and his whole demeanor changed.
"Is that what I think it is?" he asked,
pointing dead ahead.

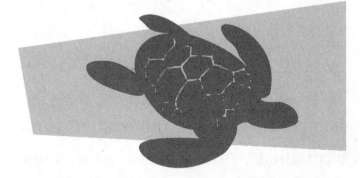

CHAPTER THREE

"Woo hoo!" shouted Bindi.

"There she blows," said Captain Washington.

Caitlin started to tear up a little. "Look at her. She's just so beautiful!"

Andy looked at his sister, surprised. "Are you crying?"

Caitlin whacked her brother. "No," she responded, wiping her eyes.

The humpback whale Andy had seen in the distance had launched herself up out of the water. Bindi explained to the twins that this was called breaching. It was magnificent. The sight of the enormous black and white creature propelling itself out from the glistening blue water was something the twins would never forget as long as they lived.

As the catamaran moved closer to the whale, they could see she was part of a pod of five adults. The group seemed to be playing together.

Two of the larger whales had calves with them.

Bindi rushed out onto the bow of the boat, taking her friends with her. She excitedly pointed out Ash and the calf. Waving her hands energetically, she tried to get Ash's attention. Ash was one of the biggest whales in the pod, and she had distinctive dark markings on her tail flukes, which made her easy to identify. It wasn't long before she noticed Bindi waving on the catamaran's front deck, and she came over and began to swim near the boat with her calf following by her side.

Bindi explained the behavior to

her friends. "That's called mugging, when the whale comes closer and circles around the boat. It means we don't invade her space, but she can interact with us if she wants to."

"She is just—" started Andy.

"...totally su-*perb!*" finished off Caitlin.

Ash responded to the compliment by diving underwater and reappearing a moment later with a powerful blow, spouting water all over the three friends.

While Caitlin and Andy were momentarily taken aback by the impromptu shower, Bindi loved it. "Nice one, Ash, you're a little beauty!"

"Umm, I might just get a little farther back from the edge," said Andy, backtracking up the deck while wiping his face dry.

Although Caitlin wanted to do the same, she considered herself the braver twin, and decided to stick it out at the front with Bindi.

After a few more minutes of mugging near the boat, Ash and her calf dived under the water and began to head back to join the rest of the pod. Bindi and Caitlin were waving goodbye to them when Andy shouted out behind them.

"Wow, did you see that?" he yelled.

"What? Another whale?" asked Bindi, looking in the direction of the pod.

"No. Way over there." He pointed farther out to sea. "It looked like a firework!"

Bindi frowned. "Really?"

Andy nodded. "Yeah, it shot straight up into the air. You can still see it coming down over there. Look!"

Bindi caught sight of a glowing spark making its way slowly toward the water. "That's bad news, Andy. It's an emergency flare, which means that someone out there is in serious trouble!"

CHAPTER FOUR

The three kids raced back up to the bridge and told Captain Washington what they'd seen.

Bindi picked up a pair of binoculars and looked toward where Andy had seen the flare.

"I can definitely see a boat out

there. But I can't tell if there's any-thing wrong from this distance."

Captain Washington started up the engines. "No worries, Bindi. Under maritime law, we have to go out there and check the boat's okay. The flare may have been released by accident but, whatever the reason, we'll go out and say g'day."

Bindi turned to the twins. "Sorry, guys. We're going to leave the whales behind for now."

"Gosh, don't be sorry, Bindi," said Caitlin. "This is turning into a real adventure!"

Now back inside, Andy was feeling uncomfortable again. "Excuse me, I might just visit the bathroom," he said, looking decidedly wobbly.

Caitlin gave her brother a comforting pat but thought it best to leave him alone. She loved teasing her brother but now was not the time.

As *Steve's Whale One* traveled farther into the open ocean, Bindi noticed something. "We're entering the shipping channel now, Captain Washington, aren't we?"

Captain Washington nodded. "Yes, this is the eastern seaboard motorway. Runs up and down the east coast. We get all kinds of ships traveling here. Trawlers, tankers, container ships—even the odd round-the-world yachtie—you'll see 'em all if you stay around here long enough."

Caitlin was fascinated. "What about pirate ships? Do you get any of those?"

Captain Washington laughed. "Not much buried treasure around these parts, I'm afraid. The pirates have to go elsewhere to find their gold."

Bindi added, "Our buried treasure is the fantastic marine wildlife we have. And, of course, farther up the coast is the start of the Great Barrier Reef, which I'd definitely consider buried, or maybe just submerged, treasure."

Captain Washington nodded. "Right you are, Bindi."

They were speeding closer to the boat, which they could now see was a fishing trawler, when Captain Washington started to chuckle. "I don't believe it," he said, shaking his head.

Caitlin and Bindi looked at him, confused. "What is it?" they asked.

He didn't answer but picked up the radio.

"*Steve's Whale One* to *Tommy's Target*, over," he spoke into the mouthpiece.

There was silence for a moment before the radio crackled its response. "You have got to be kidding, mate. All the boats in the ocean and we have to get saved by you? Unbelievable! Over."

Captain Washington bellowed with laughter.

"Captain Washington, do you know the people who own that boat?" asked Caitlin, wondering if all Australian captains spoke to each other like that.

"You bet, mate. Know them very well indeed. Actually, known them since the day I was born."

He picked up the radio once again. "What have you gone and done this time, Dad? Over," he said.

The gruff voice replied. "Nothing, son. We was innocently minding our own business, doing a spot of fishing, when some huge container ship almost rammed straight into us. We avoided a collision but got swamped by its bow wave. Now the engine's flooded. We're not going nowhere without a tow back to shore. Over."

"Righto. I can help you with that. Over."

Caitlin was busy looking at the trawler. "What's that man doing?"

A crewman, a rotund man in his fifties wearing a colorful Hawaiian shirt, was leaning precariously on the bow of the trawler, reaching down to pull in a trawl net.

"Isn't that dangerous?" Caitlin continued. "Couldn't the waves bump him over? There could be sharks in the water!"

Captain Washington looked at the crewman. "Ah, that's Mad Jake. One of my dad's old fishing buddies."

"Mad Jake?" said Caitlin with a gleam in her eye. "Sounds like a pirate name. I might go out and say hi." She headed out to the bow of the boat.

Bindi looked at Captain Washington. "She really seems to like anything to do with pirates, doesn't she?"

Andy had limped quietly out of the bathroom to see what was going on. He managed a weak laugh. "Ah, I think I know what Caitlin's about to do."

CHAPTER FIVE

At the bow, Caitlin waved before shouting out, "Ahoy there, me hearty! Is that there you trying to fall out ye olde leaky tub?"

Back at the bridge, the observers started laughing.

"Mad Jake's gonna love her,"

said Captain Washington. "I think he likes to think of himself as a bit of a pirate, hence the nickname."

Mad Jake stopped hauling in the net and looked up at Caitlin. "What did you say, love?" he shouted back.

Caitlin smiled at the chance to continue with her pirate speak. She yelled back, "You're looking like a limey landlubber out there."

Mad Jake was not used to being heckled by a British tourist impersonating a pirate in the middle of the ocean!

"Who are you? Is this one of Washington Junior's terrible jokes?" he cried, hands on hips. He seemed amused and annoyed at the same time. Unfortunately, at that moment, he lost his balance. No one saw quite what happened next, but a second later he was in the water, bellowing some colorful phrases of his own.

Captain Washington was immediately on the radio with his father. "Man overboard, repeat, man overboard."

The crackle of the radio sounded. "Typical. That bloke loves an audience. Over."

Bindi and Andy were worried about Mad Jake, but Caitlin had already sprung into action.

"Oh my gosh, I'm so, so sorry,"

she cried. She grabbed a nearby rope, tied one end quickly to the boat rail, and threw the coiled end as far as she could into the water near him. Her aim was spot on.

Mad Jake stopped bellowing for a moment, impressed. "You've got a nice throw on you, girlie." He caught hold of the end of the rope. "Got it."

Caitlin yelled back to him. "Aye, got that, matey."

By the time the other three had made their way out onto the bow to help, no one needed help. She had hauled the rope, with Jake holding onto it, closer to the boat and pulled him around to the stern of the ship. A dripping wet Mad Jake was now making his way up the back stairs, looking the worse for wear but still with a twinkle in his eye.

He shook hands with the kids and Captain Washington. Andy passed him a towel. "Where'd you pick this one up from, Derek?" he asked. "She's a natural deckhand. We could use someone like her on the *Target*."

Andy laughed. "She'd only be interested if you had a skull and crossbones on your mast, and you captained a galleon!"

Caitlin explained further. "I just *adore* the *Pirates of the Caribbean*

movies," she said. "I've loved any-thing to do with pirates ever since I was a little girl."

Bindi was distracted. "Ummm, Mad Jake, could you pass me your towel?"

He'd been wiping himself down and looked up at Bindi. "Ain't quite finished yet, Bindi. Derek, you got an oil leak on board? I can smell oil."

Bindi frowned. "It's not on the boat, Mad Jake, you're wearing it."

The humor of the past couple of minutes dissolved. "You're kidding me," he said, looking down at his Hawaiian shirt, which now had dis-tinctive dark patches on it.

Bindi was now looking out toward the bow of the trawler ship. "And see out there? It looks like there's a lot more where that came from!"

CHAPTER SIX

Oil spills in the ocean were always an environmental disaster but this coastline had even more at stake than most. Not only were the migrating whales using the east coast as a thoroughfare on their way from Antarctica to the Whitsunday Islands in late autumn and back again in late spring, this region was also home to a whole heap of other marine life: loggerhead turtles, Indo-Pacific and humpback dolphins, green sea turtles, hammerhead sharks, and sea snakes, as well as the bird life that were also often victims of oil spills.

The first thing they needed to check was whether the oil was leaking from *Tommy's Target*.

Bindi, Caitlin, and Andy went back to the catamaran's bow and surveyed the surrounding water. The wind had picked up, and they could see the ocean's current was moving more oil toward the trawler. It didn't look like the trawler had the leak.

Captain Washington's dad gave the boat a quick once-over, and their fears were confirmed. The oil must have come from a different source.

Captain Washington immediately called the coastguard and filled him in with the scant details they had.

"Got that, *Whale One,*" the coastguard replied. "I'd advise you to chase down the vessel that the trawler nearly collided with. We'll bring a boat to tow *Tommy's Target* back to shore. Chances are the oil's come from the container ship."

Mad Jake agreed. "Wouldn't be surprised."

The men decided that Captain Washington's father would stay on board his boat, waiting for the coastguard, while Mad Jake remained on the *Whale One*. The kids re-entered the bridge to hear the last of the conversation.

"Mad Jake, which direction was the ship heading? And do you remember what it was called?" Bindi asked.

Mad Jake scratched his head. "Ahh, it was definitely heading south toward Brisbane. Had a whole heap of containers on the front deck. A heavy load. And it was called something like, ah, Santa? No...Sandy? No. Sant—"

"Santiago?" offered Andy.

Mad Jake looked amazed. "That's it. *Santiago. Santiago Sun* it was. How d'you know that?"

Andy shrugged, embarrassed. "I don't know. Just a good guess?"

Caitlin interjected. "He's really good with word games," she said, looking at her brother proudly.

After passing that information on to the coastguard, *Steve's Whale One* left behind *Tommy's Target* and powered on south, traveling as fast as it was safe to go. The winds were getting stronger, and Bindi knew this type of weather was one of the worst possible scenarios for an oil spill. The gusts could carry the oil a lot farther, creating more far-reaching damage than it would do in calmer seas.

Bindi was looking through some binoculars when she spotted something dark and shiny on the ocean's surface. "Captain Washington, take a look over there," she said, pointing starboard. "There's more oil!"

Captain Washington grimaced. "Well, we're on the right track at least."

The choppy waves made the going tough, but they continued on. Soon, Caitlin pointed to a large vessel in the distance. "Could that be the culprit?" she asked.

Mad Jake squinted. "Could be."

They forged on, and the huge shipping container became more visible.

Looking through the binoculars, Bindi confirmed their suspicions. "Yes, it's definitely the *Santiago Sun*," she said. "I can see the lettering on the side of its hull. It's enormous!"

The container ship measured approximately 650 feet in length, and its cargo was visible on the deck, where hundreds of containers were stacked. Although the waves were choppy, the huge vessel glided smoothly over the water as it steamed dead ahead. As they got closer to the ship, Captain Washington tried his radio.

"*Steve's Whale One* to *Santiago Sun*, do you read?"

There was a crackle from the radio but then silence.

He tried again. "*Steve's Whale One* to *Santiago Sun*, do you read?"

Still nothing.

"We have to get them to stop, Captain Washington!" urged Bindi. Compared to the *Santiago Sun*, the catamaran looked like a tiny ant next to an elephant.

Captain Washington took a deep breath. "Righto. We're going to have to travel as close to the ship as we can and kick up a storm next to it. That'll get its attention."

Mad Jake whistled. "Kids, this is dangerous. Grab life jackets, and don't move away from the bridge. It's the safest part of the ship."

Caitlin was concerned. This had gone from being a lighthearted adventure to a seriously dangerous trip trying to stop an environmental disaster. Wait until she told her friends back home!

After putting on life jackets, they all watched the needles on the boat's instrument panel ping to the right as Captain Washington increased speed. "Now hold on tight."

The captain spun the wheel from left to right, sending up wide arcs of water on both sides. He sped the catamaran toward the *Santiago Sun*, then turned the wheel sharply and accelerated the boat away from the vessel at speed.

Bindi had the binoculars glued to her eyes, hoping to catch sight of someone on the deck. Finally, she caught sight of a crewman who had appeared on deck, gesturing at the boat angrily. "We've got their attention!"

Captain Washington tried the radio once more. "*Santiago Sun*, do you read, over?"

There was a distinct crackle from the radio this time. The group all looked at each other expectantly. Then a gravelly voice came on the line, but the transmission was unclear. It sounded like gobbledegook.

"*Santiago*, please repeat slowly, over."

Again, the same gobbledegook.

They looked at each other, perplexed.

"What's he saying?" said Caitlin.

Bindi realized it wasn't just the bad transmission that was making the voice hard to understand. "He's not speaking English, is he?" she said.

The captain had come to the same realization. He put his head in his hands and sighed. "No, he's not."

CHAPTER SEVEN

The crackle of the radio began again.
"*Sí, aquí el* Santiago Sun. *¿Qué hacé-is? ¡Podrían haberse matado!*"

Bindi asked, "So what language *is* that?"

The others shrugged.

Caitlin looked like she was about

to scream in frustration. "What are we going to do now?!"

Andy had been concentrating on keeping his nausea at bay but now he mumbled something.

"What did you say, Andy?" asked Bindi.

Andy took a deep breath. "I said, I think we should speak to him in Spanish."

Despite his fragile state, Andy's surprise announcement got him crash-tackled in excitement by Caitlin and Bindi.

Bindi laughed. "Of course it would be Spanish. Santiago is the capital city of Chile, and they speak

Spanish in Chile. Why didn't I think of that?"

Andy looked over at his sister with an eyebrow raised. "Well, Caitlin actually studies Spanish with me, so there's really no good reason why she didn't know he was speaking Spanish," he replied.

Bindi quickly intervened. "No time to argue, twins," she said. "Andy, please talk to him!"

Andy took a deep breath to steady himself and then went over to the radio. "*Santiago, ¿me recibe?*"

"*Sí, ¿quiénes son y qué quieren?*"

Andy's seasickness seemed to vanish. "Hey, I understood that.

He said who are you and what do you want?" He looked so pleased with himself he seemed to forget the urgency of the situation.

Bindi and Caitlin both shouted, "Tell him about the oil spill!"

"Oh, right. Yes, of course." After telling the master of the *Santiago Sun* he'd like to buy some cooking oil and a bus timetable (he was nervous—sometimes the wrong words just came out!), he quickly corrected himself and stumbled his way through an explanation of what had happened.

The ship's master had no idea about the oil spill and had not noticed how close he'd come to a collision with the fishing trawler earlier. He mentioned he was running behind schedule because of bad weather in Indonesia. When he muttered the word *ciclón*, Caitlin looked panicked. She might not have been as good as her brother at Spanish but she instinctively recognized the word for "cyclone."

The master promised he'd get someone to check the hull immediately for signs of a crack.

When Andy finished translating the conversation, the four congratulated him on his success. "Andy, you're a trooper. What would we have done without you?" Captain Washington asked.

Mad Jake looked around at the oil that was steadily coating a wider area around the *Santiago Sun*, now that the ship had slowed somewhat. Because of its size, the container ship would continue moving for another half hour before it could stop completely. "Better update the coast-guard on the situation. They'll send out rescue crews and spotter planes. No one knows how long *Santiago Sun* has been leaking oil. They'll need to find out how much oil is out there and how much of the coastline may be affected."

While Captain Washington radioed through to the coastguard, Caitlin asked Mad Jake something that had been bothering her.

"What would have caused a ship like that to spring an oil spill in the first place? It looks pretty sturdy."

Mad Jake thought for a moment. "Well, judging by the number of containers on the ship, they could have lost one overboard and not noticed. If it hit the hull on the way down, it could have cracked it. Could be a number of things, though. What I do know for sure is that the maritime authority will want to check *Santiago Sun*

thoroughly before it lets her travel
any farther south."

CHAPTER EIGHT

The thought of oil affecting any
marine life was upsetting enough,
but Bindi had been thinking con-
stantly about the beautiful hump-
backs that cruised the local waters.
Until the rescue crews arrived and

the oil spill had been cleaned up or at least contained, she wasn't going to be able to relax.

After speaking with the coast-guard, Captain Washington thought it best to return to Mooloolaba. He'd been in contact with the wildlife hospital at Australia Zoo, and they were on standby to deal with any animal casualties that might result from the spill. Unfortunately, this was not the first time there had been an accident like this in this area, and the vets at the hospital were experienced in dealing with oil-affected wildlife.

As *Steve's Whale One* motored back up north, Bindi and the British twins put themselves on marine wild-life duty. They rustled up another two pairs of binoculars and scanned the water, keeping an eye out for oil or any sign of movement that would indicate some type of underwater creature or bird was getting too close to the oil.

Both Andy and Caitlin were curious to know more about the effect oil spills could have on marine wild-life. Bindi told them what she knew. "Birds and marine mammals won't necessarily avoid an oil spill," she told them. "Seals and dolphins have been seen swimming and feeding in or near oil spills in the past."

"Why?" asked Andy. "You'd think they'd (instinctively) know to stay away."

Bindi frowned. "Unfortunately, some fish are attracted to oil because it looks like floating food. And this then endangers seabirds or larger predators, which are attracted to the schools of fish and may dive through oil slicks to get to the fish. Even reptiles, such as sea snakes and turtles, get caught up in the oil."

"What happens to animals that get oil on them?" Caitlin asked, still scanning the ocean with her binoculars.

"Well," answered Bindi, "it depends on a few different things.

68

Different types of oil affect the animals in different ways. Sea birds get oil stuck to their feathers, which weighs them down and ultimately stops them from being able to fly away. If marine mammals swallow the oil, it can lead to lung damage, stomach ulcers, and long-term illnesses, just like if humans swallowed it."

It was a very sobering discussion. Andy was still not feeling very well, but the situation made him feel even worse.

Mad Jake came out on deck to bring the three children cups of hot chocolate. "How are you doing, kiddos?" he asked. He handed them the drinks and noted their down-cast expressions. "Look, I know it's tough, but remember, we've probably saved a large area from being contaminated by notifying *Santiago Sun* of the problem."

As he spoke, the *whirr whirr* of a helicopter flying overhead could be heard.

They looked up. "And the rescue crews are all on their way, thanks to us," added Mad Jake. "Although that looks more like a news chopper."

"I know," said Caitlin. "I just wish we could do—"

She was interrupted by Bindi yelling, "No!"

"What? What is it?" cried Andy.

Bindi was furious. "It's Ash and her calf. I can see them swimming over there. And see over there"—she was pointing to a slick dark patch about half a mile or so from the mammals—"that's oil, and they're heading straight for it!"

CHAPTER NINE

While the twins kept an eye on the two whales, Bindi, followed by Mad Jake, raced up to the bridge to let Captain Washington know the bad news.

He was devastated. "This is terrible news, Bindi."

Bindi was in wildlife warrior mode, and she was not going to let anything happen to her precious whales. "Captain Washington, we need to herd Ash and her calf away from the area and out farther into the ocean. What if the rest of her pod decides to come near the oil? We have to stop them!"

Captain Washington nodded. "You're right, Bindi. We can do this. You try to get their attention, and I'll make sure to keep the boat between them and the oil."

Bindi raced back down to the front deck of the catamaran and let the twins know the plan. She started jumping up, shouting, and waving her arms. "Ash, Ash, over here! Follow us!"

Andy and Caitlin joined Bindi, and the three of them began trying to get Ash's attention. She'd already come over once today; who knew whether she'd do it again?

"Ash, over here. Over here."

Captain Washington started up the engine and looked worriedly over at the whales. He could see movement but wasn't sure which direction the whales were headed in.

Mad Jake switched on the loud-speaker, which was usually used to give the marine biology talk on a normal whale-watching tour. In his best DJ voice, he began speaking. "And you've tuned into pirate radio, folks, and I'm Mad Jake. We've just had a very special request come in. It's time to turn this boat into a disco. I've heard there's a special whale out there listening in, and she loves a good beat, so this one's for you and your little one, Ash."

He turned up a local radio station really loud. For a moment, the three kids wondered if Mad Jake was living up to his name and had gone a little crazy, but they soon realized he was doing his bit to attract the whales' attention.

Loud hip-hop beats sounded over the ocean waves. Bindi, Andy, and Caitlin stopped waving and started dancing. Andy's gangly arms and legs were put to good use, and it became apparent he was quite the break-dancer. He was popping, locking, and krumping like a professional. The girls were impressed and did what they could to keep up with his surprisingly funky moves!

After a couple of minutes of their hardcore dancing, they noticed Ash spyhopping a couple of yards from the bow. She lifted her head straight out of the water, keeping quite still, and watched the kids as they danced.

"Look at her!" Bindi shouted. "She's enjoying the performance. Don't stop, guys!"

Captain Washington waved to them excitedly from the bridge and started steering the boat slowly eastward, farther out to sea, making sure Ash and her calf stayed on the starboard side. The whales continued to follow, with Ash breaching now and then, definitely keeping an eye on the three dancing friends.

The marine mammals weren't the only ones interested in their dance moves. The helicopter camerawoman high above them was filming footage of the oil spill when she noticed the surreal scene playing out below her. To the sound of thumping bass, three kids were break-dancing on the deck of a catamaran while a whale and her calf were getting diverted away from the oil spill.

Incredible stuff. The network was going to love this footage!

CHAPTER TEN

Twenty minutes later, the catamaran was farther out at sea and Captain Washington gave the okay signal from the bridge. The kids collapsed in a heap, exhausted.

He'd spied Ash's pod of whales not far away, and as he suspected,

Ash and her calf left *Steve's Whale One* and swam over to be with their extended family. This far out in the open ocean, there was no danger of them going anywhere near the spill.

Mission accomplished!

Mad Jake's voice came over the loudspeaker once more. "Okay, folks, it's pirate radio wrap-up time. My little buccaneers down on the deck need some time out. Sayonara and signing out, swashbucklers."

The three kids were lying on their backs, breathing hard. Caitlin puffed. "Nice work, me hearties!"

The kids grinned.

"Hey, I think I've finally got over my seasickness," said Andy.

Bindi laughed. "If you can break-dance aboard a seagoing vessel, Andy, you can do anything!"

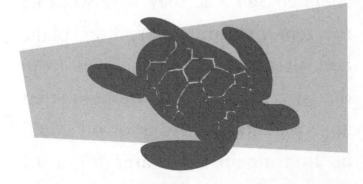

CHAPTER ELEVEN

As *Steve's Whale One* made its way back through the canals to Mooloolaba Wharf, they passed coastguard boats ready to head out and begin the clean-up operation. Captain Washington had been updated by radio that Maritime

Queensland boat was already with *Santiago Sun*, and they were working to stem the spill. A spotter plane had already assessed the area from the sky and it was thought that approximately 15 tons of oil could be floating in the water for a 12 mile stretch.

It wasn't good news, but the passengers aboard *Steve's Whale One* knew they'd done as much as they could to stop this environmental disaster from being much worse.

The kids were on the bow of the boat when they spotted Terri with Andy and Caitlin's mum waving at them with big smiles on their faces.

Terri yelled out to the kids. "Hey, we've already seen you on the TV! Nice dancing, Andy!"

Andy blushed and the three kids waved, relieved to see their families after the rough day they'd had.

Bindi turned to her friends. "Well, it's been a whopper of a day, guys," she said. "You were both amazing. Thanks for your help out there."

Andy grinned. "I can honestly say it's been the most eventful day of my life so far!" he said.

Caitlin nodded her agreement. "The rest of our holiday is going to be so boring compared to this!"

Bindi laughed. "For your sake, I

hope so!" She left them to help moor the boat.

The twins gave each other a small high five. "I didn't know you could dance like that," Caitlin said quietly to her twin.

"I didn't know you could throw in a rope and save a fisherman in under five seconds!" replied Andy. He gave his sister a nudge.

She gave him a nudge back. Soon they were back to pushing and pulling each other as usual.

Once the twins were back on the wharf, Andy bent down and kissed the ground, happy to be back on dry land. Caitlin giggled and then remembered something. She turned, looked up at the bridge of *Steve's Whale One* where Mad Jake, Captain Washington, and Bindi were waving at them.

She waved back and shouted, "Fare ye well, vagabonds. Be seein' you next time for some more swashbuckling action!"

ANIMAL FACT FILE

WHALES

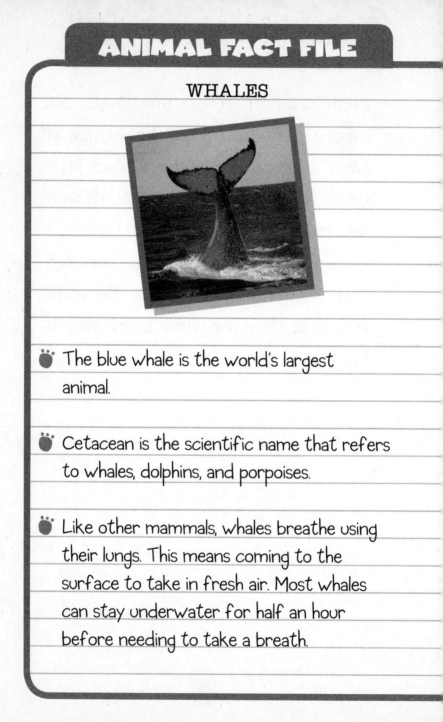

- The blue whale is the world's largest animal.

- Cetacean is the scientific name that refers to whales, dolphins, and porpoises.

- Like other mammals, whales breathe using their lungs. This means coming to the surface to take in fresh air. Most whales can stay underwater for half an hour before needing to take a breath.

- Humpback whales are known as baleen whales, as they have no teeth. Baleen are stiff, hairy sheets that hang in rows from their top jaws.

- Australian waters are home to 45 species of whales, dolphins, and porpoises.

- The humpback whales that travel up the east coast of Australia from Antarctica do so for reproductive purposes. In the warmer waters they mate, give birth, and stay with their young, feeding them mother's milk until the calf has developed enough blubber to survive in the icy waters of the Antarctic.

- Humpback whales eat krill, which are shrimplike crustaceans.

bindi
Wildlife Adventures

COLLECT THE SERIES!

TROUBLE AT THE ZOO *Book 1*

RESCUE! *Book 2*

BUSHFIRE! *Book 3*

Become a Wildlife Warrior!

Find out how at
www.wildlifewarriors.org.au

If you'd like to find out more
about stopping whaling in
Antarctica, Bindi and Australia
Zoo recommend visiting
www.seashepherd.org.

The adventures continue in

ROAR!

Turn the page for a sneak peek!

CHAPTER ONE

Bindi could hardly contain her excitement. She shifted uncomfortably in the back of the taxi. She had a very bad case of the wriggles.

Why was it that just when you wanted something really badly, time seemed to move in slow motion?

Right now Bindi, Robert, and Terri were stuck in a taxi going at about the slowest pace possible.

"Is the traffic always this bad in Sumatra?" asked Bindi, her face pressed up against the window of the taxi.

Terri shrugged. "It's my first time here, honey."

"I think we're actually moving backward," observed Robert as he stared at the traffic jam outside.

Terri gave Robert's leg a squeeze. "Just a little longer, kiddo."

Terri knew her kids were tired and couldn't wait for the journey to be over. Neither could she. It had been a long trip. Both Bindi and Robert were seasoned travelers, but they had already completed an international flight from Brisbane to Jakarta and then a domestic flight from Jakarta to Jambi.

The three Irwins looked out at the writhing mass of cars, bicycles, and general mayhem surrounding them. Boy, was it loud! The air was filled with the sound of hundreds of car horns beeping at once. It was going to be a really long drive.

Bindi willed the taxi to move faster. She had tried to explain to the taxi driver why they needed to move fast, but he didn't speak much English.

Bindi attempted to act out the reason for their visit, but she suspected he just thought she was a bit crazy. The growling and animal gestures probably hadn't helped matters.

"I don't think I can take much more of this," said Robert, his face pressed up to the window. He wanted to get out of the car and run. Kids just weren't meant to sit still for long periods of time, especially kids who were used to lots of action.

"Remember why we're here. I promise, it will be worth it," soothed Terri.

Finally the taxi made its way down less and less crowded streets before pulling to an abrupt halt outside a very ordinary-looking apartment block.

"Are we there, are we there yet, Mum?" Bindi turned to Terri in excitement.

"Are we there, are we there yet, Mum?" Robert mimicked his sister, equally excited.

"YES!" Terri grappled with the foreign currency and paid the driver. Everyone scrambled out of the car at once and piled onto the dirt road. The kids helped their mum collect the luggage. Standing before them was a concrete apartment block four stories high.

Terri checked the map. "This is definitely it." She looked around doubtfully. "I think."

"COME ON!" Bindi had one arm and Robert grabbed the other as they dragged Terri toward the entrance.

Terri knocked on the door numbered 3. It seemed like forever before they heard the sound of several padlocks clicking open.

"Goodie, goodie, goodie!" cried Bindi, as she bounced up and down on the spot.

"Ssh." Terri held a finger up to her lips. "You'll frighten them." The door opened to reveal a young man dressed in khaki with curly dark hair and a beard.

"The Irwins!" Underneath the mass of facial hair beamed a large smile.

"Cameron!" cried a relieved Terri. "Good to see you."

"Are they here?" asked Bindi eagerly.

"They sure are, the little terrors. Running me off my feet!" There was a pause before Cameron realized that the family was politely waiting for him to move out of the way. "Hey, gang, meet the Irwins." Cameron stepped back from the door, allowing it to swing open.

Bindi, Robert, and Terri clambered up the steps and through the doorway. They couldn't wait to get inside!